Hour of the Wolf
M Kitchell

<u>after James Lee Byars</u>

"They tell stories of the night..."

"They tell of desperation..."

"They ask questions that have no answers..."

"The man walked over the cliff to his own death..."

"The woman screams until her vocal chords quake in silence..."

"There's a box floating in the air, a coffin, tomb of the infinite..."

"We can hunt the void only in death..."

"We encounter death only in sleep..."

"I can't understand..."

"The crystal namesake of the earth's..."

"There is another way we can learn how to fly..."

"This is how I
hunt the void…"

"I call death my
only friend…"

"There are
shapes that
I cannot see,
colors too…"

"They tell of
men who lose
themselves to
darkness…"

"They tell of men who lose the ability to sleep..."

HOUR
OF
THE
WOLF

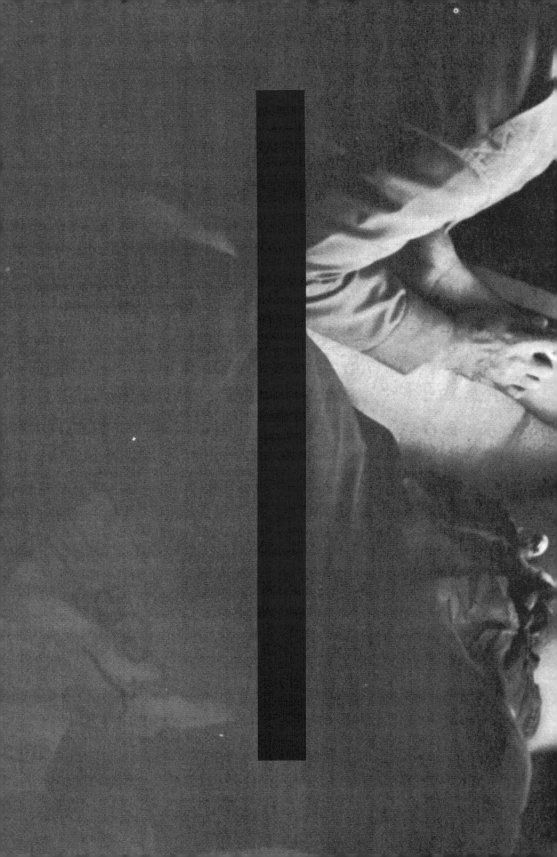

First
Cycle

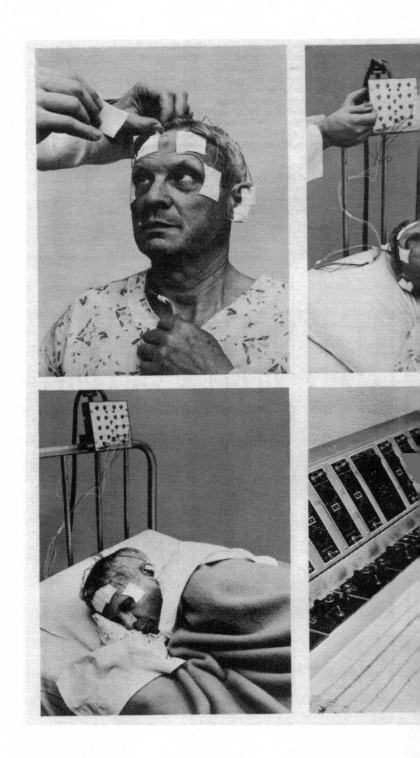

First Night

The beating of my chest wakes me up, a powerful surge, a current of space and velocity that pulls my eyes open to a pure darkness. There is no light from the street outside, any electronic lights from devices in my bedroom fail to glow, and there is such a stillness, a lack of movement that if it weren't for the fact that this had happened before, I would be unable to move.

The power is out. I'm aware of this. It seems like I understand inherently—through some pact with the energy that I circulate regularly in this bedroom, that this lack of electricity has become manifest as an exacted conclusion of some sort of physicality. A dream I had that I've already forgotten. Maybe God exists and this is His way of proving it. I don't place much credence in that suggestion.

When it happened before, the first time I awoke to discover I had somehow killed all electrical currents through a half-block radius, I couldn't move. I suffered a simultaneous exhaltation and terror: I would tremble if the night hadn't cast me in stone. But within fear I was excited—my body couldn't move but my mind fired synapse after synapse as I attempted to work out a disciplinary route towards the control of this 'power,' this potential skill that would help me gain what I wanted in the world— little more than freedom, of course.

Before, waking the next morning, I refused to accept what had happened but soon found that all the clocks in the house had been reset. No one else had been awake, so I kept my discovery to myself, and with more nights of sleep and drinking that followed it wasn't long before I dismissed the incident as a freak accident, a convergence of stress

25

and energy. But what I should have considered is more sinister: that it was an omen of what was to come, a warning.

So this time, awake, I have an idea that the lack of power is a call for me to take action. I sit up and glance around the room. If I were a different type of person I would insist that I feel an energy, a presence, but I'm still half asleep despite the jolt of awareness that brought me to consciousness and I'm far too tired to buy into any sort of speculative explanation. I can see nothing but the dim glow of the moon outside of my south facing window.

So I get up. I pull on shorts and walk barefoot over hardwood floors through my apartment, from my bedroom in the front to the kitchen in the back. I open the fridge and see that the light is out, that there's no hum. It is here that I should notice the insulating silence, interrupted only by a slight bleat of bass somewhere in the distance, but instead only become frustrated with the refrigerator which was, itself, no stranger to problems. (This detail hardly concerns you, dear reader, but as it is the first aberrant thought aside from the problematic fridge that's interrupted my mystical experience, it's perhaps worth noting.)

After the kitchen, I step outside. The night is chilly, but not impossible, California air always a welcome respite from the fringe temperatures one grows accustomed to in the Midwest. There is fog hovering through the night, shadows spreading across the moon. But to only comment upon the moon in passing would be a mistake, as it is the moon that holds my gaze, and as such, due to some ocular phenomenon I can't begin to hope to uncover, becomes larger and larger in my field of vision, pushing all liminal sight into a realm of absence, negating the rest of the world.

When the only thing in my sight is the cold yellow glow of the moon, I notice that the steady bump of bass I had heard before is now gathering grip on me: it sounds as if the beat of a drum—repeated ad infinitum with a hold so steady I can start to believe in God again—has overtaken the regular sounds of the night. As I face the extra-sensual fate I've succumbed to, ready to perform my duty to this new object of worship, this moon, a car horn honks.

Immediately, everything returns to normal: my vision resumes its depth (I can once again see beyond the flat surface of the moon), the fog parts to a normal degree of night, and, behind me, the kitchen light is back on. Inside I pass the microwave, time blinking. In my room, I pick up my phone and read the time: 3:59.

I fall back asleep.

Second Night

It comes as no surprise to me that my ceaseless insomnia has found a new way to thwart restful sleep, has decided to allow me to fall asleep quickly enough, only to then force a confrontation with consciousness far earlier than I'd choose. With repetition, thought has moved from hypothesis to proof & I feel comfortable stating that I am waking up every morning (or night, depending on one's outlook of our permeable existence on this telluric rock) at three. Never before, never after; always three. Never before four can I reach sleep again. So perhaps it's not insomnia that I should be claiming here, but it is something, and it is consistent, and it's negatively affecting my day to day functioning, I'm sure there's some clinical definition that I'm absolving myself from actually looking up, but the point is that before, with regular insomnia, I couldn't fall asleep, and now, it seems the ailment has re-manifested itself into a bizarre condition that finds me unable to be asleep between three and four a.m.

And yes, of course, three to four a.m. is the witching hour, the hour of darkness, the hour of the wolf, the single hour of every day when demons can come out and play, when the spirit world touches our own. It may be said that there are many things in life which at one point I would have found laughable, but through existence itself (and the experience that adjoins this existence), I've found myself far more receptive to what could be termed the metaphysical—mystical states that should have no place in a rational world. What I'm saying is that I immediately understood there to be some pressing urgency to the fact that my distorted brain was pushing me into the realm of the (un)real every

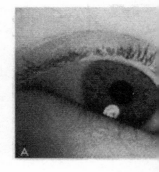

night during the hour of the wolf.

My normal response to such a repeated insistence of absurdity would be to indulge in excessive bouts of laughter—laughter at the situation, laughter at the sun, laughter at the gravity that glues me to this planet, laughter at a god who refuses the rhythm of waves to dominate my life. But I'm tired, truly, and in exhaustion there can be only a delirious cackle against the madman's howls, absent of any referent other than inner turmoil or a purely physical confusion against what it means to have a body. While it's true that I already inherently view the world as ghostlike, trapped between here and there, I've always been frustrated when these slippages take my physical well-being into account—world, if you choose to belittle me, confuse me, or throw intellectual duress in my path, I will fight you, but wear me down on the level of this poor container of flesh and I have little response available.

So, beyond this rant, I suppose it's worth delivering here what exactly happened on this second night, perhaps less strange than the first, but nonetheless important in developing the arc that will soon become apparent over the five nights detailed here for your inquiry, dear reader.

Often, the realm of chance from which one assumes to encounter the impossible is simply reducible to a complete dissatisfaction with the banal; an ennui perhaps. Within this static nature one will look for that which appears supranatural, an annulled grasp at something outside of the ordinary that can then be explained as only the impossible, something derived from chance. The surrealists were useless because they could never bring themselves far enough beyond their obsessions with dreams and vaginal intercourse to accomplish even the smallest step toward an unknown beyond.

When stepping away from the phallocentric and inherently patriarchal insistence of sex, the options generally include either an anal fixation, homosexuality, or self-hatred. All of these options, of course, are better than just being boring. Perhaps this is just decadence, but since I suffer both an anal fixation and the pleasures of homosexual intercourse I understand that God can always be in a hole but never in something like a building. And so be it to find my feet scraping the ground as I walked up and down my street in the middle of the night, or the middle of the morning, in that hour between 3 and 4 a.m.

The pleasures of living in a city—the conveniences, the culture, the business, the opportunities, are occasionally met with resistance by the others who occupy cities in a lower degree of visibility; the homeless & the poor, the men and women who push shopping carts filled with aluminum cans from one recycling center to the next, the small woman on the corner who never lets you pass without asking for a cigarette. But these people are not people worthy of scorn or shame, for they simply occupy the universe in a different mode than you. And on my street, all occupants, separated by either class or interest or simple difference always convalesced paying little mind to one another unless direct confrontation occurred. A busy street, but not a wildly violent street.

I say this, of course, to introduce the idea of how strange it was that I found not a single other living creature, human or otherwise, on the street during my jaunt. I was shocked, to be sure, as living in a center of discourse of whatever sort, the silence, a lack of voices, often contradicts expectations of life itself and the only question available is whether or not one is truly still alive.

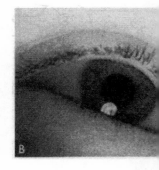

But once again I find myself veering farther into abstraction than necessary: the point is when I left my apartment and wandered the street, there was not another soul, and the absence of the living made me feel like a ghost. I like feeling like a ghost sometimes, it procures a clench in my stomach that is similar to what I feel when I dangle my body over the ledge of a tall building. This is not vertigo, quite the opposite, for the drop in the stomach, the rise of inertia through the body is something that I find more pleasurable than perhaps anything other than sex. But on this particular night, or this hour I should say, I found the feeling more oppressive than enjoyable, but I can't say why. I walked several blocks, saw trees and parked cars and not a single light on in an apartment. It wasn't quite spring yet in the city and while it never snowed it was still colder than normal, so my response was simply to chalk up the experience to a transmuted understanding of hibernation, an idea that perhaps all of my wonderful neighbors needed the rest, and if they needed rest, why indeed was I wandering the street like a madman.

Thus, I returned home.

Third Night

Through unmentionable misgivings, wonder can become wander. Knowing it's three a.m. without having to check the clock, I roll over to see if D.'s woken up as well. He hasn't. Normally he wakes up at the slightest movement, which, of course, includes any of my own.

In his sleep, I study his body, the curves of his muscle, the indentations that duvet and blanket have left on his skin. In his sleep he looks neither calm nor agitated. I place my ear against his mouth to listen to his breath. I'm comforted, but know that I have another fifty-five minutes to kill. I consider tracing his contour, running my fingers over spaces of skin that alternate from smooth to furry. To figure out what parts are cold and warm. If he's begun to sweat. It is an unusually warm night. I had kicked the blanket off hours ago, content to let our bodies warm one another.

I'm surprised that I have broken away from the touch we normally maintain through sleep. I stand up and go to the window.

Outside the night is as still as it was the night before. No one walks the street. The air is clear. I can't hear the tight-skinned drum. But I do see something on the street below my window.

It's at this point that I'm torn. I know I shouldn't leave my lover, should suffer the perpetual hour in patience, staying in bed until four a.m. hits and I can return to slumber. Something about what I can see calls to me.

On nights that I'm alone I sleep in enough clothes that the impulse to wander isn't deterred by the effort—that seems unimaginably paramount

at this point—of having to dress to leave. My skin is sensitive and often touching fabric other than clothes results in itch. A condition that I've sacrificed to the pleasure of flesh on flesh. A worthwhile endeavor. My nights become more beautiful when I'm not alone, more conducive to the rhythm of movement. I light up like a furnace when my body collides with another. D. says he likes the warmth I create.

I grab my keys. With my clothes on I slide into a pair of shoes and walk down two flights of stairs to the street. There's still no one around, but as my feet hit the pavement I think I can hear the drums. Though for all I know I'm inside—it is 3:20 in the morning and a mere twenty-one minutes beforehand I was dreaming of corridors and flashing lights. Now, in the yellow hue of civic lighting, I can see no one and my attention is drawn to a box.

I know it seems insane to imagine dramatic effect, but as I approach the box the volume of the pulsating rhythm increases. Never to the flattening point of the first night—the heavy sound that took me away as I stared at the growing moon—but to a point that's definitely beyond liminal invention. I make a mental note to ask D. if he heard anything the next morning. I wonder if he'll be awake when I return to the room.

Grabbing the box, the contents shake. I pull open the flaps and realize it's a box full of Polaroids. While it's not a huge box, there must be at least 100 photos. Perfectly square images inside rectangular frames. I start to look at a few images, can make out only Rorschach shapes in dim light, vague architectural structures, blurred ontic existence. I'm too anxious to look closer right now. I think I hear laughter.

I turn my head to look down the street.

I hear laughter.

I turn my head to look down the street in the other

direction.

Nothing, of course. There is still no one around. And, when I think about it, I realize the beat of the drum is gone (skin drum, tight skin, something that was once alive). I grab the box and return to my apartment, to my bedroom. I set the box on the floor.

D. stirs. Asks me what I'm doing. I tell him I'll explain it in the morning. I look at the clock and realize it's 3:58. I spent a half hour outside without even realizing it. What seemed like only a few minutes. I crawl back into D.'s arms, disturbed by the time-lapse. I chuckle to myself as I faze back to dream: the absurdity of alien abductee tales—always marked by missing time—floods my headspace.

| | | |

I ask D. if he heard a drum beating at any time during the night. Like, the drum for some sort of ritual, I say. D. says no and asks me about the box. I found it last night, I tell him. He rolls over, refusing to fully wake up. I climb off the bed and he moans and tells me to come back. I open the box again and start looking through the pictures. Most are blurry, but some are in focus. The blurry images look like moving bodies. The images in focus show boring architecture. Various states of decay. Factories maybe. There's nothing to understand. I keep digging through the box, intent on looking at every picture. The last image of the box is of a person, and it's the first non-architectural image that's in focus. It's a Polaroid of me. I decide not to tell D. and get back into bed.

Fourth Night

Understanding how fear operates is key in making sure that one fails to exist in the world as a victim. I find it easier to walk alone at all hours of the night, my ears covered in headphones, kept slightly separate from the reality of the world. Many people would consider this dangerous, or call me crazy, as I have never found myself inhabiting spaces in anywhere other than at-least-slightly "bad" areas. I've found that the refusal of fear is the best way to avoid inhabiting it. If one walks around looking terrified, attuned to every movement and sound, a predator is going to realize the fragile edge said person is perched upon and be all the more willing to engage with the attack. On the opposite side of the spectrum, if you walk around oblivious and totally without fear, nobody can touch you. If you destroy your fear, you become free. Without freedom, one cannot help but become a victim.

While I'm sure it'd be responsible to try to point out that I'm not saying it's best to be oblivious, but really I am. The real world is only tenable when you bother to touch it. Subjecting oneself to the real world is like signing up to be a victim. This is both true and false, because the world operates, as anyone who has been around the block more than a few times can tell you, in mysterious ways.

But really, I'd like to apologize for not telling you about my dream beforehand. Admittedly I mentioned I was dreaming of corridors and flashing lights, but I managed to leave out the entire narrative my headland fabricated before I found the box. And really, I should also note that my existence in the world has largely been predicated upon my dreams. Because of this, I know that dreams can mean many things, and certainly never have an immediately discernible finitude to them. Throughout my life, I've learned to take cues from dreams, to understand them. To know that they're not always just me working whatever bullshit banality from waking-life out in the stadium of the formless. To know that I need to pay attention to them, write them down so it becomes easier to remember them, to try to understand them.

Perhaps my hesitancy to tell the dream is a purely literary one—everyone seems to share in the opinion that reading (or hearing) someone's dream is boring, that the telling of a dream is ultimately myopic, that dreams should be kept to oneself as they show someone else nothing. Sure, this could be true, but with narrative comes function, at least in this formal arrangement where it's my words that are delivering a story to you. If you don't care for my narrative you obviously won't care about my dream, but if you find yourself interested at this point, then perhaps you'll excuse my poor form and humor me in reading on.

The dream was very simple. It began with me looking in the mirror and noticing, after turning around, claw marks on my back immediately above my ass. Claw marks, I say, but a better description comes by way of event: consider a large bird landing on the square of my back and digging in; not deeply, but deep enough to leave a mark, a few steps, and then flying away. This situation can describe the marks I could see in the mirror on my skin. Marks that trace the confused path of a lost bird.

The phrase <u>to misunderstand sand</u> heaved through my head in the dream, pounding with a steady repetition, as if the words had replaced my pulse. After looking in the mirror, lights started flashing and I found myself walking down an endless corridor. As I continued my walk I carefully noted the walls of the corridor. There was little light in the hallway, so my estimation may be off, but the walls seemed dark, a cool marble, swirled gray like ash, lead. When I finally looked to the floor I saw

dirt. My feet were bare.

Ahead of me I saw a flash of movement, the corridor lighting dimmed and I stilled in my position. I felt the dirt beneath my toes and dug my digits deeper. With such disorientation undoubtedly about to occur, I wanted to literally ground myself. With flashing lights I could see parts of a large bird, gray and black like everything else in the space I was walking through. The light never permitted me to see the entire bird at once, only fragments. I soon realized that the bird was flying toward me.

Unwilling to be made sacrifice to this prehistoric creature, I turned around and ran, dirt shaking beneath my feet. The flashing continued. In front of me dim light began to reveal obscured architecture (though not entirely similar to that found in the Polaroids from the box that existed in waking life, similar enough to find me placing emphasis on this fact in recollection). The irregular flashing became even more casual in its execution. Light and dirt swirled into one, a sweat of material and light. I wanted to understand the bird that had marked my back like I wanted to understand god. The light took over, the corridor stretched out ahead of me, and it was in that moment I woke up.

This was, of course, last night. Tonight, waking from sleep at 3 a.m., I left no dream. I woke up casually considering the idea of sand, perhaps an echo from the dream of the night before, but nothing definite. I was cold. I didn't want to leave the apartment because of this cold. The erratic weather of the city was beginning to get to me, an absurd abjection washed over my body. Alone this time, I stood up and began pacing in my room. I grabbed my cigarettes and walked back to my porch.

Smoking, in the past, was something that I had used to fight insomnia. It's not exactly pleasant, in any capacity, but it certainly offers something to actually do while one is exhausted and sleep seems impossible. I would take drags deep into my lungs, exhaling them as slowly as possible, a sort of perverse yogic exercise aimed at hypnotizing my

brain into finally succumbing to sleep. Tonight I wanted only to confront a banal exercise instead of letting my head run wild into the bizarre circumstances that had been repeatedly haunting the hour of the wolf.

I walk out to the porch & the light—automatic, set to detect motion—that I expect to come on fails to do so. I move in the general vicinity of the light to wave my hands, careful not to run into the jade plant on the deck beneath the light. Still nothing. I mutter "fuck it" to myself and light the cigarette. In the dim glow of the lighter I notice something sitting on a stump of wood in the far corner of the porch.

As I walk toward the dim shape I stub my toe on something. Reaching down to pick it up, I hear a flutter of wings ahead of me. I click the lighter and see that the wooden stump is now bare. I grab and feel cold marble. Under flickering light I examine the stele, cold gray in color, heavy and smooth like marble. There's an inscription of some sort set into the face, but I can't make it out in the dim light. Putting the stele in my pocket, I finish smoking my cigarette.

Inside I turn on a light and hear a voice whisper that the stele is a cenotaph. There is no one in the room, I feel like I must have imagined the voice. My finger runs along the impression, I can feel the letters Q, R. The next line: O, Q. The final line: Q, D. The question of the room, the one question, the question of death. These ideas are not mine either. I turn off the light and let silence hover.

Final Night

I wake up in the damp of my own piss and find that there's someone else in the room. I realize it's not piss I've woken up in but blood. I'm not in my room. There are multiple people around me.

Masked figures, nude beneath black cloaks, faces obscured by murkily transparent cloth.

The skin drum beats, bleats, hit hit hit.

The rhythm is disturbing so close, there's something off about it. Something inside of it doesn't make sense. It beats with a pain, it lacks an actual rhythm. I'm inside of the sound and find myself irritated. I don't care about the blood, I only want to get out of the sound.

I'm on a wooden floor in front of a larger copy of the marble stele I found the night before. The light is dim but looking at the layout of the room I'm in, I'm reminded of my own apartment. I realize I'm in the apartment beneath mine, empty after a fire sometime last year.

The fire. Nobody knows how it started.

Four polaroids are laid out in front of me, presumably positioned so as to face the four cardinal directions. To the north, a photo of the scars on my back, the scars that only existed in dream. To the east, myself in profile riding the bus. The glass between my body and the camera reflecting a flash of light. To the south, my body lounging in sun. I can't figure out where the image was taken, but I'm sure that the body is mine. To the west, that path I've never bothered understanding, is my body laid out on the ground, nude. The photo is from tonight, taken where I am right now.

There's no blood in the photo.

The blood can't be mine. I feel fine.

My body feels fine, my skin.

I'd touch my lower back to make sure that the dream-marks are gone, but my hands are tied in front of me. I feel a cold breeze and understand that I'm naked. I wonder where the blood came from.

I'm on my side struggling to look up at the people around me. They walk in circles. Despite nudity I cannot see sex, the figures are indiscernible. All I can see is smooth. Smooth flesh under black velvet.

I try to speak but my throat is too dry. I have no sense of time, but assume the worst. The worst or, arguably, a single rooted fact that I can hold onto: it must be shortly after three a.m. I hear the fluttering wings of a bird.

As if the figures can read my thoughts, they part themselves into two rows to reveal the room ahead of the room I'm in, separated only by alcove, no door. What I see is not a bird, but more of a winged human-like figure. I feel something. Something is welling deep inside of my body, a darkness that understands all architecture is useless, that the diversionary tactics of language can't hold a candle to the world's secret reality. This is strange information to try to deliver like this. A heaviness.

The figure slowly, painfully, stands up. Feathers clumped in viscera fall to the floor like ruffled flesh. The sound that comes out of the figure's mouth is horrible. The voice refuses gender, is barely human, but speaks in a tonality that I can understand. Speaks beyond language, insists only on sounds. I wonder if this is what god sounds like.

It is at this point that I realize what the figure is. An angel.

Though, at which point in descent? Is this angel freshly fallen from the heavens, or an angel who has spent time below, working its way back to argue with god? I listen to the distorted moans of communication.

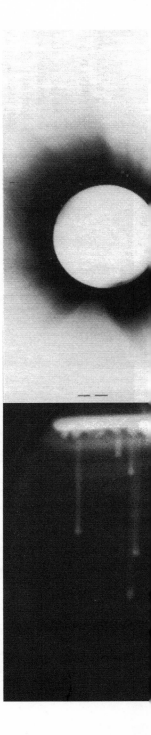

HHHHHHHHHHhhhhhhhhhhhhhhhhhhhh
(I understand this moan to indicate the nature of my current experience, my thrust into the night, this insistent location between three and four a.m., indeed the hour of the wolf, the lycanthropic anthropomorphism of angels, between birds and dogs, wolves, but more human than a human could ever be)

hhHHHhhhhhhhhhHHHHHHHHHHHHHHHHHH
(With this sound, which I swear I can see as the color one finds at the apex between blue, gray and brown, the angel tells me that it's all over, that my flesh will only be spared if I can solve the enigma of difference between one angel and the other. I realize I'm being forced into solving a puzzle, that this entire experience—of which I've kept my own emotional response out of so far—is only play, a game for the bored angel who now, I know, must be waiting for its opportunity to finish his ascent towards the heavens, to seek retribution)

At this point I'm terrified. My body is frozen and I continue to stare.

HHHhhhHhhHhhhhhhhhhhhhhhhhhhhhH
(I realize that if I can stay present, or alive, or whatever exactly, until four a.m., that I will be spared from whatever consequence is planned. The angel could come back, but I feel like were I to succeed, the damaged pride would keep the angel away. There's very little at stake in this event, at least for the angel and it's cabal)

hhhhhhhhhhhhhhhhhhhhhhhhhhhhhhhhhhhh
(The angel prepares to deliver the enigma I must solve)

hHhh, HHHHHHHHHHHHHHHHHHHHHHHHHHHH
(A sound that resolves with so much reverb I can feel my body shake)

43

HHHHHHHHHHHHHHHHHHHHHHHHHHHHHHHH
(the sound, endless, I can feel nothing but the
sound, I can see nothing but the apex of color)

HHHHHHHHHHHHHHHHHHHHHHHHHHHHHHHh
(and the question has been asked. The question
being:

QR, OQ, QD

The same letters from the stele, I consider what the
voice floated last night: the question of the room,
the one question, the question of death)

It wasn't an answer the angel wanted, but another
question. There was nothing to solve. Only
something to ask. I could think of nothing. Any
question that came to mind was only immediately
relevant to the situation at hand: Why am I here
right now, whose blood is beneath me, why did
you appear to me before as a bird, what does the
hallway mean, what do the lights mean, where do
you come from.

But I only get one question, and this question
has to be the answer, the solution to the puzzle, so
I brace myself and refuse to speak.

The angel floats colors in intense sound at
me, an aural assault, I fear becoming deaf but still I
insist. I understand the question now.

The question is of silence.

Second Cycle

Sand

N discovering—there's not much to do around the town at night—there's only an excessive moaning that can be heard from caverns below—caverns below the city, tossed like wild stones polished in the river—these caverns that hold the moans, that surround the city—N wants to explore them, but is afraid—N is afraid because at night he does not understand how he ends up places sometimes—he sleepwalks, you see, N sleepwalks, and beyond that—though distance is up to argument here, but beyond that, yes—beyond that, N suffers sleep paralysis—like the time N woke up to find himself surrounded by men in robes, maybe not men, but something, surrounded by a group of individuals staring down—N could not see their eyes and this is where the stress found its locus—he couldn't see their shape, their form, yet still he couldn't move—but his father told him the next day it was a dream—but N understands that in dreams you are not terrified: if you are terrified in a dream, that dream becomes a nightmare—and N knows that nightmares work in different ways—yes, because N understands nightmares.

Yes, because N understands nightmares—but this doesn't mean he enjoys the nightmares, rather it means that somewhere in the back of his head he is prepared for them, ready to accept them—perhaps even to embrace them, to make them his own—perhaps even to craft a new reality out of them, a reality of suffering located further into the 21st century instead of the 20th that the town refuses to leave behind—but perhaps we're getting ahead of ourselves here, as poor N has just discovered, at this point in the story—poor N has encountered the fact that he keeps waking up every morning at 3 a.m.—at 3 a.m., the hour of darkness—and cannot fall back asleep until 4 a.m. at the earliest—no, not just not fall asleep but literally cannot do anything but ensconce himself in the shell of darkness offered by the icy wilderness of the hour— this hour of darkness, the excessive moaning heard from caverns below—the ice, the ice—in the caverns however there is something else, there is a muted floor, this floor not dirt but sand—dark sand, everything is in darkness at this hour—and N finds the sand very comforting, enveloping even—for, as the hour gets closer and closer to 4 a.m., N finds himself sprawled on the ground in the cave—for the cave is deep enough beneath the ground to be warm, away from the ice— and on the forgiving sand N finds himself

    falling

        asleep.

        But before this we should examine the hour of the wolf where N found himself awake— the hour preceding his slumber at the hands of sand in those warm caverns beneath the town—the town that echoes its own name in darkness, beneath the darkness, within the darkness—what's with this darkness, some might say—but there is only this darkness—the horses sleep at night in wooden homes with latches on the doors—this is good because around here the horses show their teeth and kick like god would kick if he could walk on our land as a magnificent being instead of as a man—as a creature who is powerful—unlike N who is a simple man who occupies a simple task during the day, the task of being the town's poet, his role to explore words and fabricate beauty, to tell other townspeople what is beautiful and what is not, this is the role of a poet here—unlike N who is very good at his job and satisfied to have little other to do—unlike N whose sleep paralysis, coupled with an apnea that sets his dogs on edge as he feigns sleep all night—unlike N who is a man who we can understand because he is only a man, not a god—N our protagonist hero who has just fallen asleep in the cave, but we've diverted ourselves away from what was at task here, the hour, the lost hour of night—the night in darkness this night:

N wakes up unsure of why he is waking up. Unable to immediately fall back asleep, and glad to be free of the iron-grip of sleep paralysis that haunts him on many nights, N decides to take a walk through his small town. In the town he can see nothing, but he hears moans coming from caverns located on the south side of town. The south side of town is covered in ice, but the caverns are beautiful and as a poet N understands beauty. N walks toward the caverns and the moans grow louder and louder, but the moans do not bother N. The moans, he assumes, are only the creaking ice in the wind, the movement of the earth under feet. N is not worried. Upon reaching the caverns N discovers the beauty he was hoping for, dim in the slight illumination of reflective light: the moon, the stars, but deeper there is more warmth, and a phosphorescence that illuminates the caverns, creates an entire system of god. It is here, in the dim glow of the living, that N returns to sleep. He encounters nothing that indicates the moans were anything other than what he perceived them to be.

Melt

The moaning becomes a part of N's subconscious—try as he might, it never leaves his head—he considers it floating as something like tinnitus, something that perhaps in a few years doctors will be able to repair—but he realizes that perhaps he should listen better, actually try to hear the moaning, perhaps try to discern individual voices—but the functional aspects of such a task become difficult when faced with all the noises of daily life—there is no stillness in the town, for the town is busy in industry—there is only a reason to lay back and ruminate on beauty, his job of course—but he finds his job difficult with his haunted ears—he decides the best thing to do is to take the sound to task, to route it inside of the earth, discover where it comes from—and thus he takes leave of his desk facing the sunny window, his plants and his rocks, the gentle vibrations of the earth, and heads back to the caves.

His walk is not a long one, but N doesn't understand why things take as long as they do sometimes—he never really gets why pleasure can't be easier—what N doesn't understand is that pleasure is already easy, it's living that's hard—regardless, N makes his way to the caves, looking at the sky as he walks (and perhaps this is why it takes so long, it could be said that he dawdles)—there's nothing in the caves today in the sunlight and he's confused—N knows that he left his sweater in the cavern this morning upon waking, he loved that sweater and really never wanted it to go anywhere—that sweater that a lover had knit for him once, a gentle man with a calm demeanor that both understood and couldn't deal with N's predisposition to beauty, the necessity of it—not everybody is able to love a poet, and this reflection, which now hovers above N's mind, makes him regret leaving the sweater—but still, he decides since it is light he will walk further, he walks further toward where the luminescent organisms lit up his nocturnal jaunt, and finding himself tired once again deep into the cave he decides to take a nap, a rest, just to provide himself with the energy to return, not longer than a half hour—and of course N sleeps for hours and hours, when he wakes up the sun has set. ⋮

⋮And so N makes his way out of the cave in the dark, he is confused because the sound has ceased, the moaning stopped—he's fine with this at first, but he has realized, in this absence, that he did not give himself the proper opportunity to understand the moans, and this inherently bothers him—him, a man attuned to the poetry of life, fulfilling this role in society, he begins to question his success as the town's poet—but soon this self-deprecation dwindles because he realizes he cannot find his way out of the cave—that the cavernous tunnels he had used to source the organic light have shifted, as if the entire cave itself is alive, moving and breathing like N himself—but that's ridiculous! he insists—he knows he should insist this at least, but as a dreamer it's not as if he hadn't considered the potentiality of sentient landscape—but as if to interrupt his own train of thought, a new sound enters N's head, a sound of running water. ⋮

⋮ The thin stream runs water and N runs alongside it—this water a calm, gentle belief, he thinks—this water bringing life to these caves—and it is within this thought, this thought of life, that N realizes he has become cold, cold in the dark of this cave's night, without the sweater a lover had knit him, without the comfort of knowing he is not alone in the world, that he is loved, without all of this, in a coldness, N falters—stops alongside the water, the gentle stream, the calm stream—knees to the ground, his position as if he were to start praying, a misunderstanding ! he shouts—but this is no misunderstanding—and soon recognizing that desperation is far from beautiful unless examined under a peculiar lens that N himself lacked, he pulls himself together, wipes his eyes with his dirty hands, points his eyes to the cave walls expanding above him, and pauses—a gentle pause like the gentle belief— an attempt to gain focus, an attempt to remember something, perhaps—a something that would help him—his arms raised to his side, he is calling to the sun that he cannot see, that is in all reality below him at this point—and there is static :

: there is static
but after this static we find N back in his room with his beautiful plants and rocks—he has clearly found his way home—how, we perhaps know not, but that is unimportant at this point—for now, having returned to warmth and light and the glow that is happiness—this glow that warms the room around him—we can find N finding rest, falling asleep, asleep in his bed, much more comfortable here than during his nap earlier in the cave—here N finds rest.

But what :

: does N dream of :

: but what does N

dream of :

: and how long does N dream:

N dreams of the caves, this fact not surprising, but in this dream the caves are not rock but ice alone, huge tunnels and paths in a structure made of ice, a palace, god's organic effluvia. Inside of the caves N finds himself facing a pool of mercury. He first stares into the pool in order to admire his own reflection, but, quickly remembering the story of Narcissus, he looks beyond his own gaze, refuses to lock eyes with his silvery double, and instead stares deep within the pool. N's vision fogs and it seems that he falls into the pool of mercury, but his skin is not burning, his skin is not gray, his body is fine. His body feels as if it's floating in the murk. The feeling is good, the feeling is beautiful, so he focuses his eyes to look deeper into this mercury that he can now not escape, this mercury that envelopes him like the womb. He feels the totality of existence and in front of him sees a group of people wearing robes, surrounding a small cairn.

Emptied

The small cairn is what he can find in the caves the next day—no longer surrounded by people in robes, no longer haunted by the smell of burning wax, no longer a hovering terror—only a cairn, this pile of rocks, N finds the pile of rocks beautiful, he stares at the pile of rocks, he pulls out a pad of paper and begins to sketch the pile of rocks, this beautiful cairn—N's drafting skills are only slightly less than his skills as a poet, his skill of shaping beauty in the form of language—all of this ridiculous, he thinks, as he confronts the contradictions of his present reality—this oneiric confusion he's recently suffered—this insistence against and toward sleep—he fails to understand how it all evens out, he fails to understand the cosmic unity, the osmosis of things as they shade from one realm to another— and in this failure he continues to sketch, filling page upon page with drawings of the rocks from different angles—this cairn, he feels the air of the cairn, he feels it like one would feel a religious object, how one would feel in front of their own altar—this cairn, he says to himself, shall be my altar.

And so he contemplates the altar, and the deeper his gaze burrows into the space of the cairn's aura the more he realizes the futility of his position, his position in the town, his position of cataloging beauty, of presenting it—this realization haunts him more than the hum—this realization being a strike against the dream of his own life and a step toward what he always hears others refer to as reality— and so, the drawings of the cairn laid out in front of him in a grid, he walks around the grid, N watches the grid, all the images, all lined up, he walks back and forth, up and down, between the columns and rows, and in the center is the actual cairn itself, the holy cairn—N realizes that his drawings are nothing in comparison to the cairn itself—they are not objects of beauty like the cairn—the drawings are only ephemera, mere representation, the representation missing the hold of the object itself—the drawings miss out on the holiness that the cairn itself contains—

N becomes angry.

N becomes angry.
N becomes frustrated in his anger, and he pulls a box of matches out of his pocket, a box of matches he always found beautiful in its simple geometric proportions, its functionality, its utility, and so he strikes one of the matches and sets one of the drawings on fire, and with that fire, the fire engulfing that sheet of paper, he continues to spread the fire over the other drawings, letting the fire spread from one drawing to the next, creating a blaze in the caves, and as the images burn up, as papered ash floats into the air, the cairn remains stoic, it sits in the center and seems to almost observe the flame—the cairn remains unmoved—and in this stillness N reaches an understanding—he reaches an understanding and within this understanding he comes to a decision—but the decision is shelved for now, because his decision, N feels, is less important than continuing further into the caves, the cairns, he realizes, have spoken to him and suggested this, the cairns have suggested that he go deeper and farther—the cairns want him to plumb the depths, because the cairns are telling N that there is even more he fails to understand within his isolation, his poetic isolation—all a fucking ridiculous sham, N realizes—and so he leaves the burn behind him, letting shadows guide his path, smelling the faint burn as he walks down and down, though perhaps he is not moving down, only forward—but in this forward movement he is walking away from that which he knows and understands—following shadows like a map, until the shadows stop, until the scent is gone, until N has forgotten

the shape of the cairn.

But it is here when

57

N smells a new burn, an infinitely stronger burn, deeper, further, N continues forward, the light comes back, there is a pit, a huge cavern presents N with a pit, and deep into the pit there is a flame, a flame that N did not create—this flame is infinite, N immediately understands this—this flame is eternal, this flame is god, this flame is where creation came from.

N looks deep into the pit, he can see something moving deep within the pit:

N can see the witch-dance of a large white serpent, writhing in boiling heat, a screaming hiss escaping through the flame, worse than the sound of a boiling kettle, the sound of a screaming pain, an infinitude of pain, and N becomes very afraid. N becomes afraid of the white serpent in the pit, beneath the flames, this white worm. N, terrified, walks backward away from the pit, through the path he has entered, until he can no longer hear the cry, until he can no longer smell the burn, until the new shadows are gone. And it is here than N turns and runs, runs back to the cairn, kicks the cairn over to see it shattering in the pile of ash, and runs out of the cave until he is back at his home.

Release

The next day N walks to the city center and tells his superiors he is abandoning his position as the town poet.

There is no difference between A & B.

N sleeps all day and refuses to go to the caves.

Still, N dreams:

→ 　　　　　　. 　　　　　　, 　　　　　　　　　　　　　　　　　　,
　.　　　　　　　　　, "
,　　　　　　　. "　　　　　　　　　　　　　　　　write this
down in the green notebook, 　　　　　　. 　　　　　　　　　.
,　　　　　　　　　.
　　　　　　　　　　　　　　　　　　　　　　, "　　　　　　"　,
　.　　　　　　, "the movement of
the figure 　　　　　　　　　　, 　　　　　　　　　　　　　"
　.　　　　　　　　　　　　　　　　　　　　　　　　,
　　　　, 　　　　　.　　　　　　　　　　　　　　　&
whispering he loves you
　.　　　　　　　　　　　　　　　? 　　　　　　　　　　,
,　　　.　　"
　　　　　　　　, 　　　　　　　　　　　　　　　　　　"
　.　　　　　　　　, 　　　　　　　　　　　　　　　　.
,　　　　　　　　　　　　　　　　　　　　　　　　　　"
"　　　, 　　　　　　　　.
　　　　　　　the way the body sits,
　.　　no
　　not only,

: "
,
,   ."
, "   "   ,
,
. An unexplained absence   ,
; "   .   ,
.   .

,
.   says, "It's time to leave."
,
,   ,   ,
,   ;   "   .
;   "   "
, "   .   ; rapture
of the night,   .
                    moving clouds,   :
!   ,
,   .   .
:   .

                                                  ,
                                                  .

            ;   "   "
        "no, he loves   y o u,"
.   ,
                                                  .

                              .
                                                  .   .
.   .   ,   ;
,   .   the   false
songs of night's howl   .
        ,   .   ,   ,
—   —   ,   .
            ,   , "death is an accident."   .
                    !

        .   ,
                    a dampness,   ,
        .   .

no   ,   .
"   "
                    ."

;   ?
Death as observed by victims,

                                             .

                          ;   ,
        , "   ."←

With the dream ending, N feels as if he has opened the door to encounter his double, posed with a knife to slaughter him and take his place.

N walks outside and stares into the sun.

N stares at the sun until his eyes can see nothing but white light and his head pounds with an immensity unmatched by anything but the core of the planet earth, beating with the desire of an end.

Excess (Or, Escape)

Despite his aggression, his tired sense of worth, N returns to the caves, N knows he needs to re-confront the pit, the burning malaise that has brought him such ennui, in an attempt to come to terms, to make an understanding, to know what it is that he's doing now, such a state of the impossible

It is easier now, in his repeated trips, to move around the caves, to ignore the shifting light and shadows, the way temperatures move from warm to cold with little notice, he walks deeper and deeper, finding specific arrangement of shadow, like the topology of a kingdom of a forgotten god, N knows he has once again reached the burning pit, for he smells the burn, the infinitude.

N sees the serpent above the flames this time, N stalls in terror, N sees the serpent crawling alongside the pit, through the flames, out of the pit, circling the well that encases the pit, the serpent, this white worm, creating a perfect circle around the hall.

N sees the snake bite its own tail and still. N sees the snake bite its own tail and still.

In a solid position the white worm resembles gargantuan statuary, the snake's pale skin, gray in the shadows, resembling a solid cool marble, and this statued snake begins to hum, a gentle hum that N finds very appealing, the hum of something definite, a gentleness similar to that of the stream which N had encountered days before, and in the same way N felt it necessary to feel the water of the stream, N finds it necessary to feel the skin of the snake. ⋮

⋮ N touches the snake.
N touches the snake, running his fingers and palm against the smooth skin, this white worm, and as N continues around the perimeter of the well, the pit, letting his hands continue rubbing the smooth skin of the snake, images flash in front of N's eyes, N fugues into terror ecstasy and sadism, the images in front of his eyes both excite and terrify him, N is coming to terms with the entire realm of experience, N understands there are images communicated by the gray snake, this white worm, communicated through touch, this is why the snake has stilled, the images cover his eyes and he can no longer see the great hall of the caves, he can only see the images given by the snake, feel the smooth rough skin of the snake on his hands, smell the burning of flesh I mean rock. ⋮

⋮ But what is it that N sees:

The images N sees move in a flicker over his eyes, as if he is being blinded by the projection of film. Images move from one to another via quick cuts. There is no connecting tissue. The images make N feel like he's slowly broaching the edge of insanity, he feels like his eyelids are disintegrating in a pool of acid, or lava, or the flames of the pit itself. The first image N sees is a young boy, terrible mutant horses, four of them, surrounding the boy. The young boy is nude and, in the background, behind the mutant fauna N can make out the black-robed men and women of his dream, faces indeterminate, the boy starts to scream. The mutant horses, faces echoing the melt of plastic, malformed into expressions of agony (for the emotional lives of animals are a mystery to humanity outside the realm of the impossible). The boy's arms and legs are each tied to a different horse-like creature. N understands that the boy is being quartered.

Despite having no wish to see the operation, N realizes, as the chanting of the black-robed figures heightens in intensity, that he now has no choice, he cannot cease feeling the snake, and so in front of him in terror and horror the nude boy's small limbs are torn from his body, N hears bones break and blood begins to appear, the horrible sounds of everything around him. And after this death a new death is presented, this time a body being unjustly mutilated by a snake-like creature—snake-like in form but bearing six pairs of tiny legs, the snake's head (this snake not at all like the solidly still white worm of touch) burrowed into the figure's hole, mouth screaming in a register unmatched by the most extreme limits of any knowable musical instrument, the snake periodically pulling his head out to reveal organs and blood and flesh and what's inside of flesh hanging out of its mouth before violating again, until the violently pulsating body stills and the screams stop. Next there is the terror of a thousand children being set aflame by a horrible dragon, but N refuses to believe in the fantasy of dragons and can't understand what this creature is, something untouched by the literature of fantasy, something far more horrible, the sight mixing with the smell of burn in N's reality creates the atmosphere of pure death, burning death. A final scene presented to N's eyes is that of his own death, or destruction, perhaps not a death but a simple tearing apart, N sees his own body nude on a stone table, an altar, there is nothing in the air but he understands the robed figures are near, his own body on this stone table altar presented to a god of something horrible, something never understood by man, something too terrible to be expressed in language, and inside of his own body, which N sees in front of him, he sees his flesh quiver, move, a viscera of flesh like a puddle, under his flesh there is life that is not his own, there is something slowly tearing him apart from the inside, like a sense of being buried inside of another body, and at a pure moment of fright N watches the small worms, toothed & horned like demon-beasts pop out of his flesh, he can hear himself screaming for he knows this is a slow death, the tiny demonic worms missing his essential organs, keeping enough blood inside of him via a system of digestion that takes the essential sense of life out of what the creatures eat only to return it to his body and as he waits to see his own death completed before his own blank eyes, N's hand reaches the large white worm's head and the images stop.

N opens his eyes which he didn't realize were shut, finding himself face to face with the white worm, an evil looking animalistic grin almost, a purity, really, and the snake opens its mouth, emitting a slight hissing sound, and N stares into the snake's horrible fangs, ready at this moment to die, to be sacrificed to this mythical creature in the cave of his own undoing, but instead, the snake only mutters a phrase:

"You're ready now."

N's eyes, which are gripped tight, once again, in fear after the snake's utterance, open to see there is nothing ahead of him but a new path on the other side of the well, on the other side of the pit, a new path which N had not seen before, and looking at the ground N sees a slough of dirt where the snake had once lain.

N walks through the new hole and finds a stream again, deeper this time, he lowers his body into the stream and lets himself drift down the path. N, floating on his back down this gentle stream, deep enough for the comfort of the float, watches the ceiling of the cave as he moves downward, he knows it's downward, away from the town with his job which he has abandoned, away from the sleep he has failed to adequately ride for the last week, away from any and all responsibilities he once had, on this ceiling the bio-luminescence returns, arbitrary marks left by the living fauna and flora of the cave (for N cannot be sure which), and as the light shifts N recognizes more a thermoluminescence, realizing that it is the cave indeed which is alive, and the heat of the earth he's being brought deeper into is making the light grow brighter and brighter, a brightness suggesting that of a second sun of the hollow earth, but without another thought N's body is deposited into a large estuary, beneath him N can feel the slight brush of fish and eel, and N knows what he is ready for, he is ready for this return, this womb.

N's body floats out to sea, and N is never seen again.

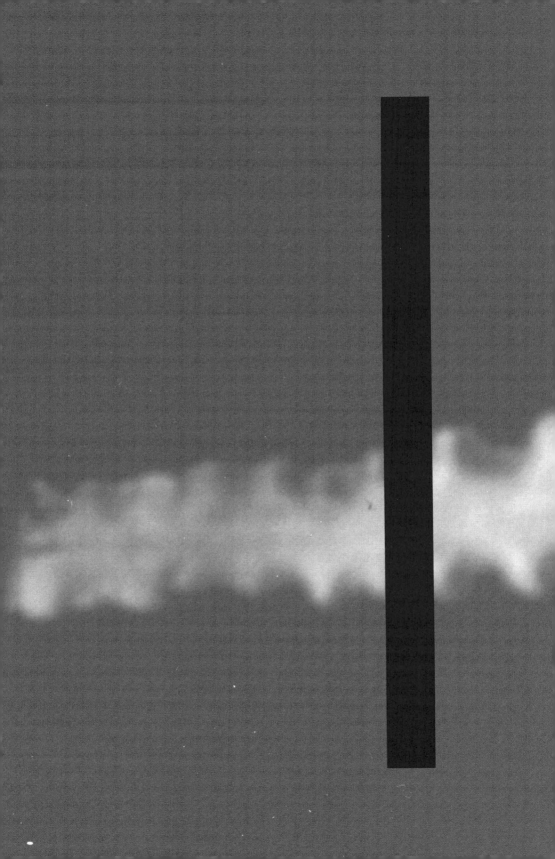

Third Cycle

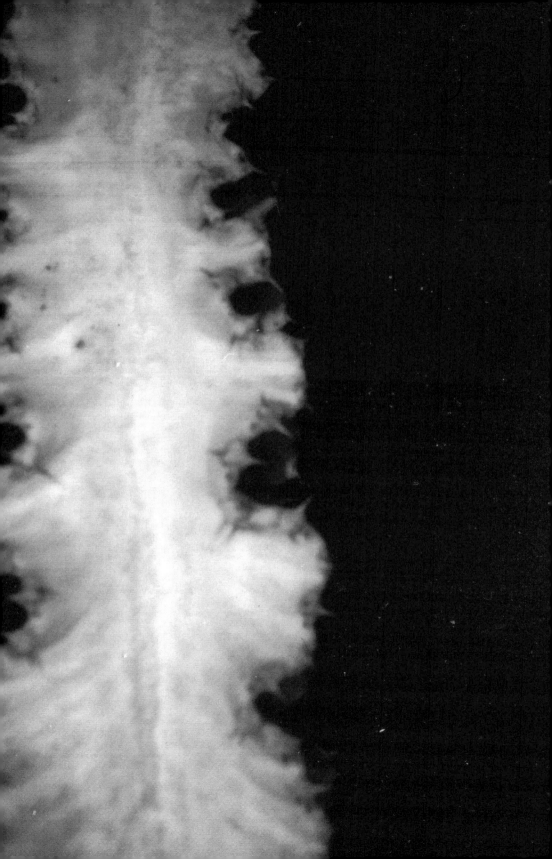

01

The man wakes up in sweat it's the middle of the night he quickly looks around his room: wooden paneled floors; small pyramidal pile of sediment—sand mixed with dirt mixed with other telluric ground—; candles in excess pushed against the wall, all not burning; large half-geode, open to the sky, perhaps usable as a chair; heavy black curtains pulled over a very large window that spans almost the space of the wall; the Euphorbia lactea cv. WHITE GHOST that towers seven and a half feet into the air at it's tip, the tallest tip at least, several other small appendages curving off into blank air. Everything is how it should be there is no sound there is no fire there is only the expectant room of his the room that the man sleeps in every night that the man works in during the day. There's a heavy silence in the air that the man can't help but notice a heavy silence that seems thick and opaque like muddy oil covering a ground or wet gravel waiting to dry in summer heat this is what the air feels like the man thinks and as he comes to this realization as he faces this heaviness his breath starts to jump his lungs constricting he is having an asthma attack and he's not sure what to do so he stands up very still in the dark and stares at the ghost euphorbia, symbolic of the virility of death that he keeps to remind himself of inevitable futures, the man stares at the WHITE GHOST and shuts his eyes focusing very carefully on his breath and how it modulates in and out in and out several years ago he thought that regulated breathing was the key to levitation an unending desire to watch his body float several inches in the air but that practice came to an end when nothing but disappointment could be detected in all reasonable venues in which he chose to research. The man is focused now he feels like his blood is pumping in tangent with the Euphorbia this succulent that overwhelms him in stature this plant that fills the space of the room like god fills the air in the desert. Time passes as the man continues to modulate his breath, moving in and out with the consciousness of the WHITE GHOST, until after an hour the man is fine can return to his low-sitting cot return to sleep.

02

The start again of waking up when one has only the desire to be asleep this time for the second night in a row the man finds himself far more concerned though still tentative about any new idea of reality. The man lights several of the candles scattered about the floor allowing smoke to fill the room and blow out of the window he keeps slightly cracked at all times, and in this this new aura the man approaches the Euphorbia lactea focuses on it in attempt to attain a confluence of mental energies because—see, the man is convinced that the euphorbia is a sentient being that could, realistically, in a demonstration of the virility of death, kill him in his sleep—he knows the WHITE GHOST has something it wants to tell him. The man reaches his hand toward the euphorbia to pull a strand of thread away it must have risen from the cot and in the gentle breeze of air landed on the plant he pulls the thread away and a quick movement the sound of something outside of his bedroom door finds him turning too quick his finger the left pointer is gripped by a small spike the man mutters under his breath and pulls his hand away too quickly for the spine of the ghost has penetrated the finger. The man can feel the euphorbia's sap mixing with his own blood, his insides moving like the way sound and light travel through space, like sonar, a bouncing a mixing like the egg into zygote or really a deeper understanding of the hermaphroditic sexual act perhaps how the Acera's witch-dance attracts a mate so the insides can string out and the new can light the deep transparencies of the sea. Or maybe it's just like being pregnant with god, the man thinks to himself, now in a succulent-inspired mania, he's lost control of his own body, drops to the ground and crawls around until all the candles he had lit are blown out, smoke hovering

into the air the man thinks he's developing ghost vision
I mean WHITE GHOST vision I mean Euphorbia lactea
vision he sees a haze and understands it as sap in front
of his skin of which his eyes are everywhere. The man
collapses onto his cot and can finally go to bed.

03

The night air is cold and as it hits three a.m., the man has just reached a deeper level of sleep. The candles in the room are all still burning, for the man does not fear death by flame. In consideration of becoming one with the Euphorbia lactea (aka becoming a ghost) he is no longer concerned with death—though it is likely that the rest of the inhabitants of the building the man lives in would be very concerned to hear of unwatched candles burning late into the night. But the man of course wakes up with a start his breathing fine this time but something else about the space confuses his eye's sight the WHITE GHOST towering over him immediately he is convinced it is closer than before bending in new ways in new shapes that seem to droop as if the sentient ghost wanted to walk on the hardwood floors of the room the man spends his time in. Tonight will make more sense, the man mutters to himself as he climbs out of bed desperate from a lack of sleep but he is convinced that as he becomes one with the euphorbia his mind will resort to a sort of hibernation when the winter months hit a static rest that will erase all ailments of man the furor of cries faced by bodies in pain, tonight will make more sense, the man mutters to himself again his clothes all pulled off as he arranges the candles in a circle around himself the euphorbia and the sediment, he removes the bandage from his finger and lets his ghost blood drip into the pile of earth and he touches his own flesh his sex becoming engorged from the half-state of dream he had just barely entered the geode sparkles outside of the circle with the reflection of the flame and the man on his bare knees on the bare floor about to reach orgasm the man in a heightened state begins to understand that in front of him the euphorbia is offering a soft pulsating glow like the light of a hovering craft from another planet or even dimension the euphorbia's glow makes the man feel like something new is happening inside of his body as he comes closer and closer to reaching orgasm the plant glowing more steadily now ready to understand the offering the mixture the man comes and the come falls onto the pile of dirt and without any action of his own the man now doubled over in true sexual exhaustion sees the viscous fluids in the pile of dirt mixing on their own accord the blood and the semen and the dirt he notices them vibrate and shake and the candles all at once go out smoke hovers into the air and in the darkness the man knows the fluids are still moving because the euphorbia continues to glow and the euphorbia is like god watching the man and it is at this moment that the earth begins to violently vibrate the earth quakes and for a moment the man is afraid of the euphorbia falling and crushing him with its collapse but as the candles all knock to the ground the euphorbia stays glowing strong from a blue to a white light and this white light begins to overtake everything the earth never stops shaking and the man can only see white.

04

(At morning, everything in the man's room is fine. The candles are not in a circle they are still placed against the wall the earth is not muddied with come and sweat and blood, the euphorbia stands at attention. The day is long and busy and the man does very hard work on various tasks that he hopes to complete in as short a time-span as possible. The man, however, feels very tired from the nocturnal adventures that have been imposed upon him for the last few nights. After the day is over, the man falls asleep exhausted.)

The night is very warm and the window is open the window blows the curtains of the man's window into a waving pattern a sort of beauty based on gesture and precise moments of spatial relationships like cephalopods birthed into the sea this light float in air like what it must be like to watch god pirouette. The candles are not lit and the man is naked, asleep in his bed. As a church clock in the distance strikes 3 a.m. the man wakes up once again suffering a quest for breath, brought forth by his own dream's questioning of repeated events the salacious nature of nocturnal emissions versus nocturnal adventures and if it really can be an adventure if it's rather exhausting instead of exciting and how does language deal with all this and when it's dealt with how does this affect reality beyond language. The man cannot breathe. The man jolts up forced to face anxiety of his brain functions diminishing due to lack of oxygen an acute sense of disorientation and confusion and the realization that everything in his room is gone the candles gone the pile of earth gone the geode gone the Euphorbia lactea cv. WHITE GHOST gone the curtains on his window gone. Everything is gone and in everything's place there is only a large white marble sphere placed directly in front of the window, the window that once was covered by thick curtains now open to the air which has stopped moving for there is a hyper-sense of stillness and outside the world has blurred into the haze of cloud and fog and in front of this haze of cloud and fog the white marble sphere sits upon the wood-paneled floor of the man's bedroom. The man walks to the sphere. The man touches the sphere and lets the coolness of the sphere take heat out of his hands. Because he cannot breathe, and because the room is hot from the stillness of the air, the man places his nude body entirely on the sphere, embracing the smooth stone and what it feels. The sphere is gentle and calms his breathing, the man loves the sphere for this reason. The man's eyes are shut and within the coolness of the sphere he begins to think he is falling asleep but the blackness he encounters is not the back of his eyelids in the dark it is only the space around him a pure darkness still the marble sphere beneath him carrying him healing him like only perfect geometry can and soon the man's eyes begin to adjust and as he stares around he finds there are no spatial elements to put his position in any sort of perspective, there is no depth where he is for he seems to be floating in space, hovering in blackness while embracing the white marble sphere. The man questions his existence, then simply wonders if the WHITE GHOST managed to open up a black hole in his bedroom, manifested in the form the white marble sphere that has allowed his body to reach perfect, and now this black hole this empty depthless space is the palace of perfect that the man will now forever inhabit.

05

In the timeless space that the man now inhabits floating still on the white marble sphere which in flight could perhaps be considered an orb given that it seems incapable of suppurating itself to the laws of nature as in gravity in this timeless space yes the man wakes up and because the space is timeless he cannot be sure of whether or not it is at three a.m. that he finds himself awake. He knows only a pleasant sense of calm similar to that of a prolonged orgasm, as if he had sought out and achieved a stillness through a history of study and ennui only to encounter that the secret of life's pleasure is a floating feeling better than any imaginable or unimaginable sex. His body has become one with the sphere and the man is no longer worried about losing his breath because he has shed his body and thus needs no longer to breathe. An effervescent sense of fulfillment of all bodily pleasures sensation overtaking the world and removing all sight sound touch smell taste in lieu of something total a totality of perfection something that cannot be accurately depicted with anything short of the new death a new idea of surpassing the body into the impossible.

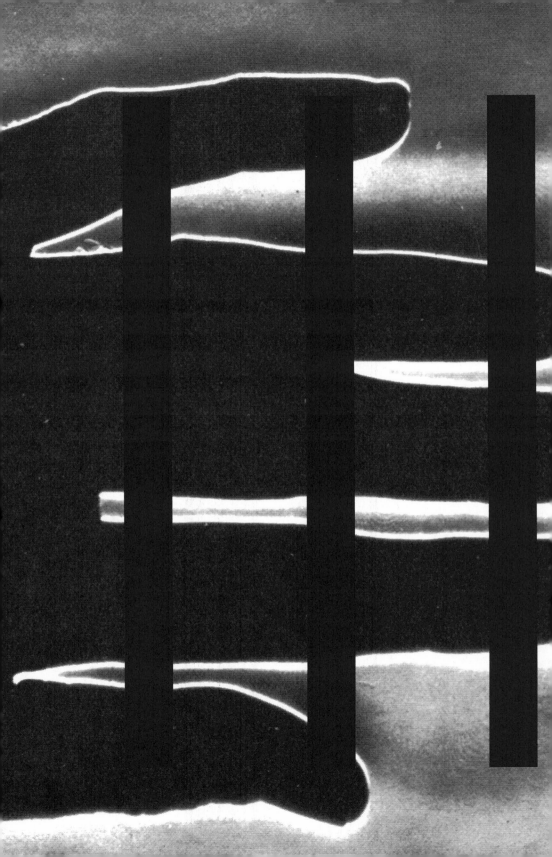

Fourth
Cycle

00:00-24:00

You're the off-season groundskeeper for the <u>maison</u> and it's in the middle of nowhere. Desert heat. Dry air. As if the dust itself is too tired to shake in wind. Not that there's any wind. Heat covering the walls like sweat. Can't believe the paint hasn't peeled. The <u>maison</u> is beautiful, like a palace. Decadence lives in all corners of the earth, even where no one visits. But they do visit, the people, during the winter. A winter palace. A palace of perfect. The architecture makes little sense to you. You want to hear voices cycle through the corridors, watch plays performed on the stage in the large hall. You sleep in the last room on the second floor. There're four floors. You're having trouble sleeping. You always have trouble sleeping. Like days and nights rolled into one when the landscape surrounding you can't differentiate other than going from dark brown to light gray. No idea how color works in this flatness. Every night you ache. Desperation. There's a necessary feeling you don't know how to shake. Loneliness. This is what sleep brings. You drank all the alcohol in the first month, it was the only thing that would help you. Now you're just stuck.

03:00–04:00

Time seems problematic when you have little to do other than make sure dust doesn't blanket the home. Home seems like the wrong word. The palace of perfect. The <u>maison</u> where you've rediscovered desperation. Your attempt at holiness brought to a halt by exhaustion. As the sun rises you sit on the parapet and practice breathing. Focus on the easy geometry of the structural necessities around you. When you wake up it's the middle of the early morning, the end of the night. 3 a.m. in a time-zone that you're still not sure makes any sense. Difference. You walk to the window and the endless sprawl of surrounding looks exactly the same, only flatter in darkness. You think you hear melancholic chords underneath the voices that aren't there. While you can't sleep you play a cassette recording you made of static. This is the only calm in the desert at night. If there were animals to protect the palace from you'd at least have something to do. Focus. This is all there is. Enough food to last the remaining months at least. A fat paycheck. You can't think of everything at once. You don't understand how within exhaustion your body still refuses to be asleep. If the <u>maison</u> were a pyramid at least you could impale yourself on the tip. Maybe. Death can't be much different than this ennui. The only thing that reminds you of your own body is how slow it works. Fall asleep an hour later while the tape continues to hum noise.

19:30-03:00

The sun sets slower in the desert. You can see for miles, or at least it feels like you can. There's nothing in the way. You try to invent stories of abandoned children struggling to exist—not in any reality, but in this empty space that you see out the window. The palace is beautiful but you don't understand it. You don't understand perfection. As the sun begins to set you walk directly out of the maison's front door holding an iron rod. The rod drags on the ground and creates a straight line. "I'll walk until the sun is gone," you think to yourself. You get too tired before it happens. You pick up your rod and move it an inch parallel to the first line before you return. "This line is a dividing line. This line is all that exists between me and god." You understand god even less than you understand the palace. The first month you lived here, in this desert, you mapped your path through the hotel until you had exhausted the labyrinthine hallways. This is when you started to play the voices in your head. The voices of the others, those that take holiday in this place. The way winter turns the rich into intellectuals. The one time they read a book. You've read all the books you brought with you multiple times already. You thought you could write but it seems you've forgotten how. Time still slows. When you wake up at the same time you can't move. Your eyes dart around the darkness for an hour or so. Nothing changes. You're afraid you're dead. When you wake up the next morning you curse the fact that you're not.

03:00-04:00

Three a.m. three a.m. three a.m. three a.m. It rings out in the darkness as you wake up again. This time you return to the parapet and stare at the sky. Darkness. You could swear that something stares back. You think you feel a breeze but you know that's impossible. You look to the east to try to watch the sun peek over the horizon but it's still too early. But this is when you see the man. The man is far away but without even knowing any defining features you feel nothing but love for the man. You want the man to tell you stories, to love you back, physically and emotionally. He won't. He can't even be real. You're barely real yourself. But the man keeps walking. He walks to the garden of obelisks where he pauses. You think you can see his mouth move but it's still too dark to be sure. You try to shout out but find that your voice is absent. A void. The man's hair reaches his neck and his beard is thick. His eyes are beautiful and haunted. You still can't see this of course. You walk down through the palace to the front door where the man stands directly in front of you. You wonder if he's holy. He slowly strips himself of his clothes. They drop silently onto the sand. He leaves each item of clothing next to a separate obelisk. His nude body is beautiful. He might be god. He takes you in his arms and you begin to cry. Taking your head in his rough hands, he puts his mouth next to your ear and speaks: "check the false doors, this palace is a tomb. Help me." You stare him directly in the eyes and understand oblivion. You want to follow him to the abyss. Instead you only lead him to your bed.

07:00-...

In the morning your body feels good. Your flesh pushes against the man's, whose fur rubs against your own. The man wakes up, tells you to remember what he said, and walks out of the room. You return to the parapet to watch him. From above, you see him pick up each piece of clothing one by one and put them on. After he is fully dressed, you look at the sun. When your gaze returns to the man he is standing atop a palmiform column just beyond the obelisks. The man is holy. You watch him glow. You want three a.m. to return forever. The singular hour spent with the man will become the most important moment of your life. An escape from the excess of reality. A calm outside of ennui. Satisfaction met in every capacity. The man is a saint and his presence is in remembrance of your sins. You walk around the palace to find all the false doors. One of them turns out to not be false. Inside, you shut the door behind you. You close your eyes and lie down to die.

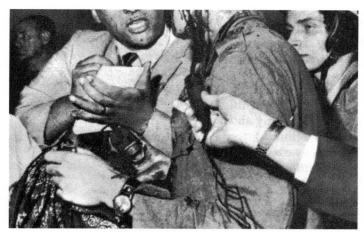

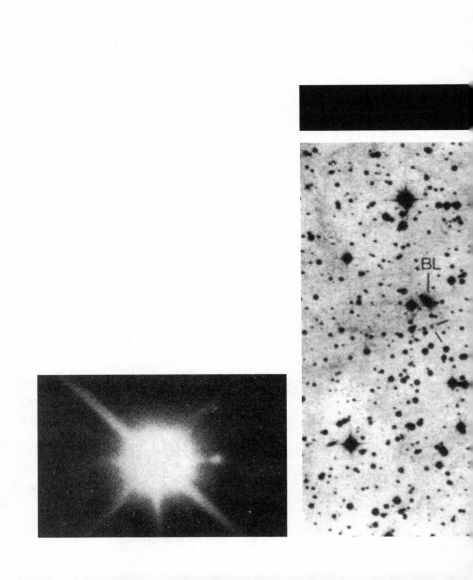

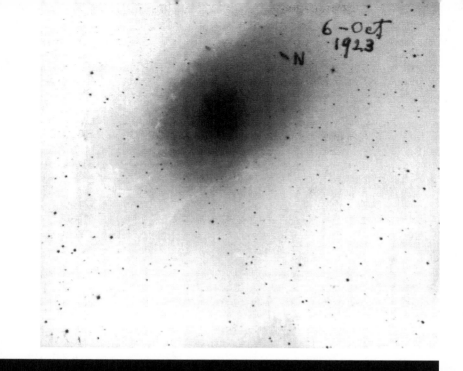

6~Oct
1923

N

Final Cycle

To confront the double
as a subject of aggression
this line of sight

night | dreams

the only sight of darkness

river rocks | current | bubbled air | emptiness | thought, this

and
still there is
another, another of
those wandering sounds
dirt

SOON

the skin of the leopard   one of many this doubled
                                           line of sight from A to B
                                           but not the only places of
                                           the dark

THIS HOUR, TOO LONG

outside in the darkness, the dark of the double
inside of the night, this dreamscape of worth
word of suffering, warning, active space of night

THIS HOUR, THIS DREAM

cardinal insistence   absented nature   no
no   insisted upon as the being of cards   like tarot
                              no   the apse

COLLIDING PLANETS IN THE ATMOSPHERE
A LANDING ON DIRT NOT OF EARTH

                                           gravity

The Cycle

ANGELS OF LIGHT
and night

the only thing

[black cube   ]

this tomb   the ancient dream of totality

making a mark on the paper, the cenotaph, this vessel containing
nothing, synthetic nights and pain

[sphere, cube, pyramid, stele]

dawn
day
dusk
& dark

SYNTHESIS
THIS TOMB

Tide

dawn

1

the mediumistic capacity of the sacred geometry
intersected by the importance of clairvoyant vowels
within the construction of absent integrity that of the
sun and the float not telling the future but predicting it
the left side of the volume dedicated to the past, the
right side dedicated to the future, the spinal gutter
understood only as the present spheres can always
float the cube structures itself to the earth

3

day

dusk

2

electronic voices permeating airwaves of lost halls
the space of wandering without moving forward,
always having to be somewhere unmitigated ennui
the pyramid points toward god, or [   ]
these rooms and hallways a map of language a heap
the stele sitting on the circle of stand, direct lineage
introduced between the sky and the earth melting is
not the present, only an excuse only an excuse

4

dark

Earth, Opened Up

and still it is said that the book can shout.
the stone book upon the earth this pedestal.
the stone book of all
truth and lie side by side
a falsity of velocity

language stone

a depth in the opacity

this all   all this

nowhere

NOW, HERE

exact

o
f

a
l
l

that can be remembering
remembering time delineated
spaces opening up

left   center   right

if only   the earth

a diagram   in the sand   if only

this can all be remembered
the past tense
the present a void

no spatial connecting tissue

only a gasp for breath

lightning
　　thunder
　　　　rain
　　　　　snow
　　　　　　sleet
　　　　　　　hail

down
down
down
down

EXCESS
TAKEN
AWAY

thought forms from light
of cloud rain thunder'd scent

A SECRET, ONLY JUST

no one is answering the questions
no one is asking the right questions

the encounter of　　　　　｜　　this double

the mirror labyrinth

                    we save all thoughts
                    and put them into
                         action

WRITE THIS DOWN

                the action of light and sound

                the non-action of language

                                not an indication of color

        the spaces of float

        these spaces of float that are life

        this insistence on hovering above

        the air the water within

        the ground pushing like

                                THE GROUND PUSHING LIKE

                    this sense of feeling

                    the stage, this page of white

                                a white sea, a white death.

white sea

white death

Hour of the Wolf
M Kitchell

ISBN-13: 978-0692787434
ISBN-10: 0692787437

The original version of this text was written in February of 2013. Text was revised and heavily edited in September and October of 2016. The earlier version of this text was first published in 2013 in an edition of ~30 from VOID EDITIONS. Each book's cover featured a golden square painted by Dean Smith.

Edited by John Trefry,
Designed & typeset by M Kitchell

A text from Inside the Castle
http://insidethecastle.org

"The gateway to the invisible has to be visible." —René Daumal

Made in the USA
Columbia, SC
21 November 2017